MAR 1998

3880 BL98

Property of:
Center for Children/Young Adult Books
College of Education
Mankato State University
Mankato, MN 56001 Property of:

D0886672

backhoe excavator

boom

cab

backhoe

crawler tracks

cab

flatbed truck

cement mixer

cab

chute

pulley

skip truck

steering wheel

seat

hinged skip

crawler crane

cab

crawler tracks

motor scraper

cab

For Lisa, with love   S.T.

For Peter   A. A.

ERC
Juv.
TH
149
.T344
1998

Text copyright © 1997 by Sue Tarsky
Illustrations copyright © 1997 by Alex Ayliffe
All rights reserved. This book, or parts thereof, may not be
reproduced in any form without permission in writing from the publisher.
First American edition published in 1998 by G. P. Putnam's Sons, a division of
The Putnam & Grosset Group, 200 Madison Avenue, New York, NY 10016.
G. P. Putnam's Sons, Reg. U.S. Pat. & Tm. Off. Originally published in 1997 by ABC,
All Books for Children, a division of The All Children's Company Ltd., London.
Published simultaneously in Canada. Printed in Hong Kong.
Text set in Stempl Schneidler Medium.

Library of Congress Cataloging-in-Publication Data
Tarsky, Sue. The busy building book / Sue Tarsky ;
illustrated by Alex Ayliffe—1st American ed. p. cm.
Summary: Shows what happens on
the construction site for a new office building.
1. Building—Juvenile literature. [1. Building.]
I. Ayliffe, Alex, ill. II. Title. TH149.T344 1998
690—dc21 96-53153 CIP AC
ISBN 0-399-23137-4
1 3 5 7 9 10 8 6 4 2

THE BUSY BUILDING BOOK

words by SUE TARSKY

pictures by ALEX AYLIFFE

G. P. Putnam's Sons

New York

site hoarding

skip

cable drums

site hoarding sheets

concrete slabs

flatbed truck

construction site cabin

REPORT HERE

building plans

site engineer

safety officer

site inspection report

bulldozer

backhoe loader

dump truck

tipper

protection barrier

general foreman

drainage pipes

steel drums

barricade tape

Ready, set...

Before construction can start, the site is boarded off to keep pedestrians out.

The site engineer checks the measurements against the building plans. The construction cabin goes up, working machines arrive, building materials are delivered, and the workers in their helmets move in.

Excavate!

Workers dig a big hole for the foundation, or basement, of the building. The foundation will provide a stable support for the entire building.

rubble

skip

motor scraper

mobile crane

hinged skip

general foreman

backhoe

skip truck

architect

plans

site agent

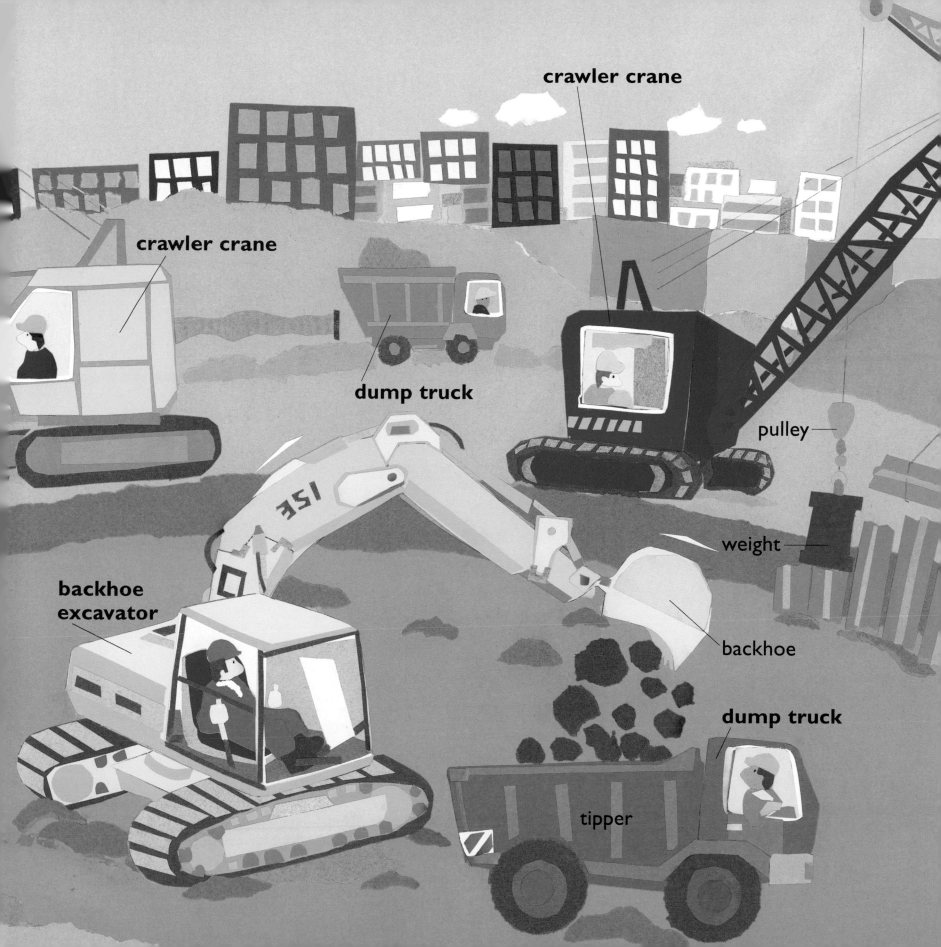

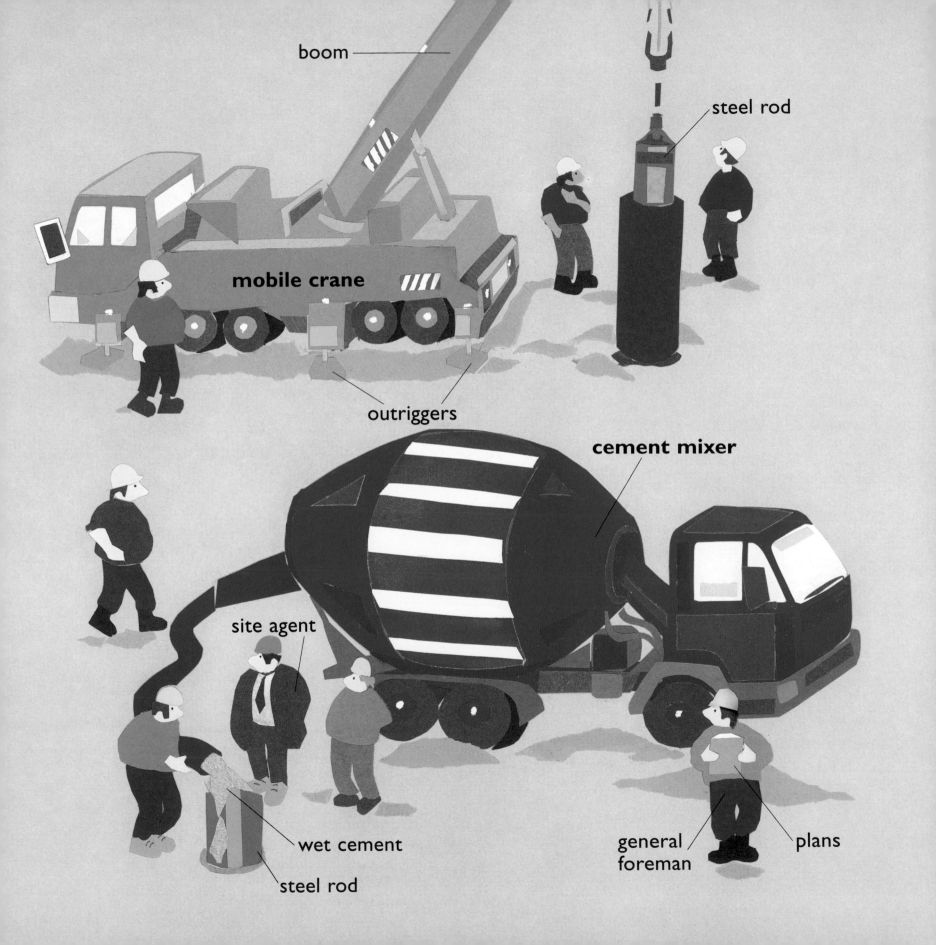

boom

steel rod

mobile crane

outriggers

cement mixer

site agent

wet cement

steel rod

general
foreman

plans

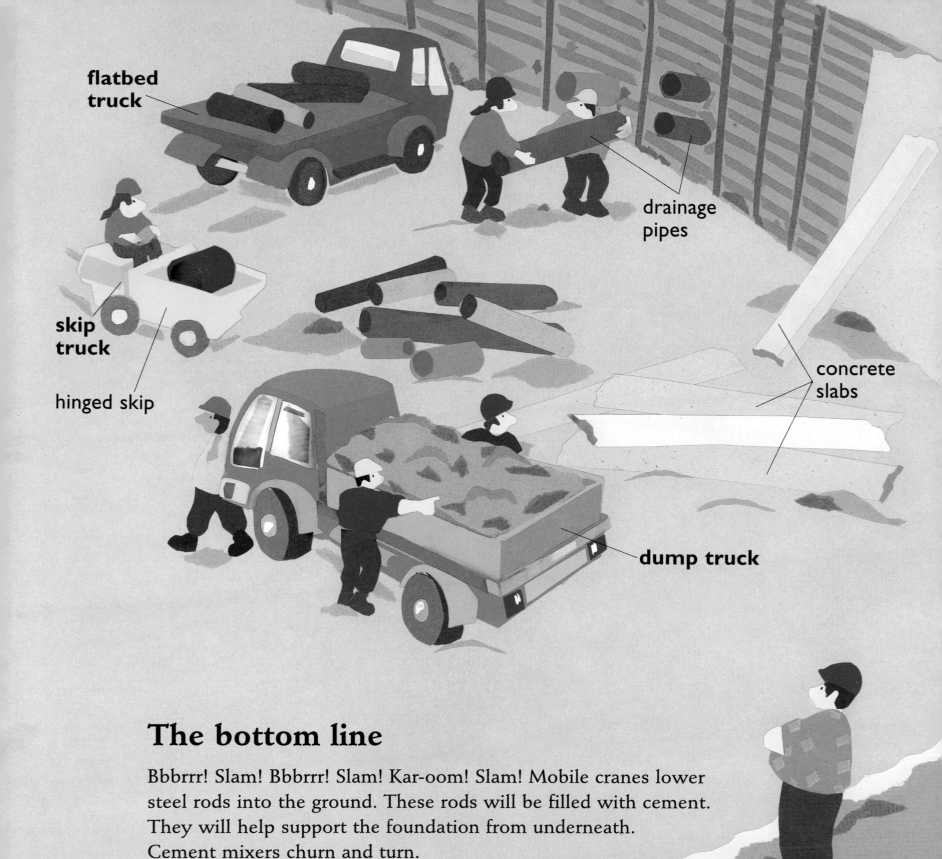

flatbed truck

drainage pipes

skip truck

hinged skip

concrete slabs

dump truck

The bottom line

Bbbrrr! Slam! Bbbrrr! Slam! Kar-oom! Slam! Mobile cranes lower steel rods into the ground. These rods will be filled with cement. They will help support the foundation from underneath. Cement mixers churn and turn.

Going up!

After the foundation is done, workers build scaffolding. The scaffolding is a temporary platform for workers to stand or sit on when they work higher up. Pedestrians stand and watch.

backhoe loader

dump truck

scaffolding

site hoarding

tower
crane

backhoe
excavator

delivery
truck

dump truck

skip truck

DANGER!

KEEP OUT!

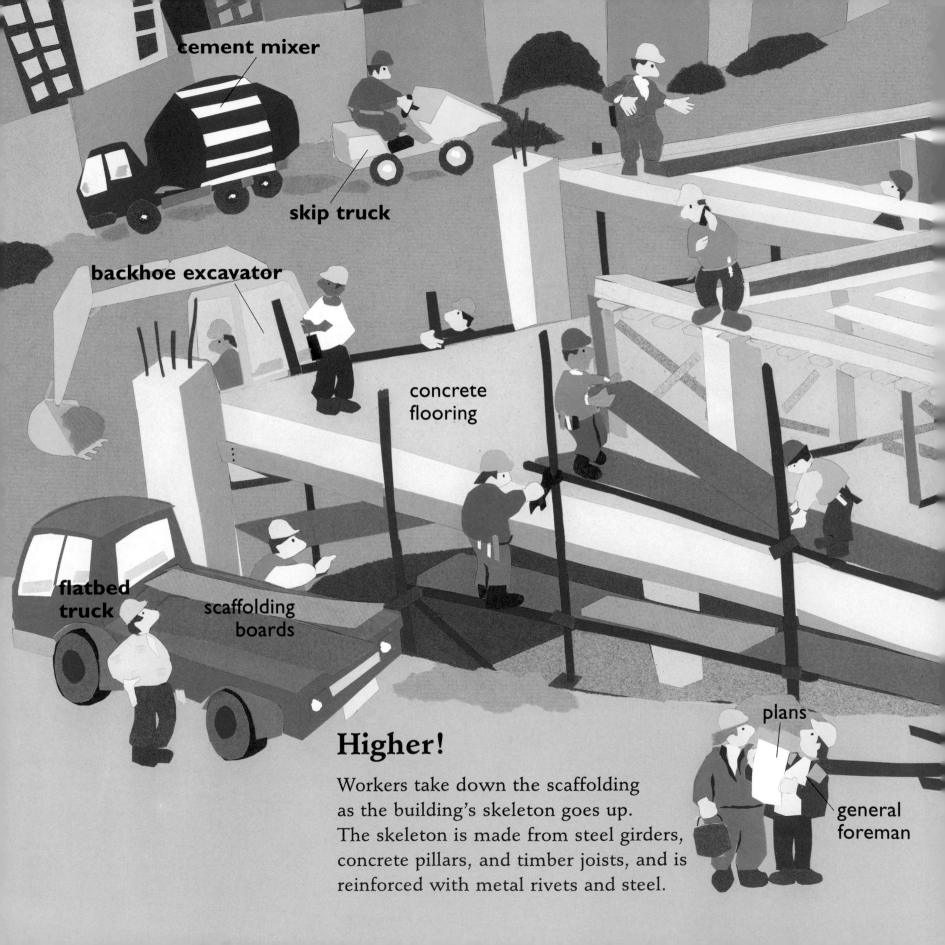

cement mixer

skip truck

backhoe excavator

concrete
flooring

flatbed
truck

scaffolding
boards

plans

general
foreman

Higher!

Workers take down the scaffolding
as the building's skeleton goes up.
The skeleton is made from steel girders,
concrete pillars, and timber joists, and is
reinforced with metal rivets and steel.

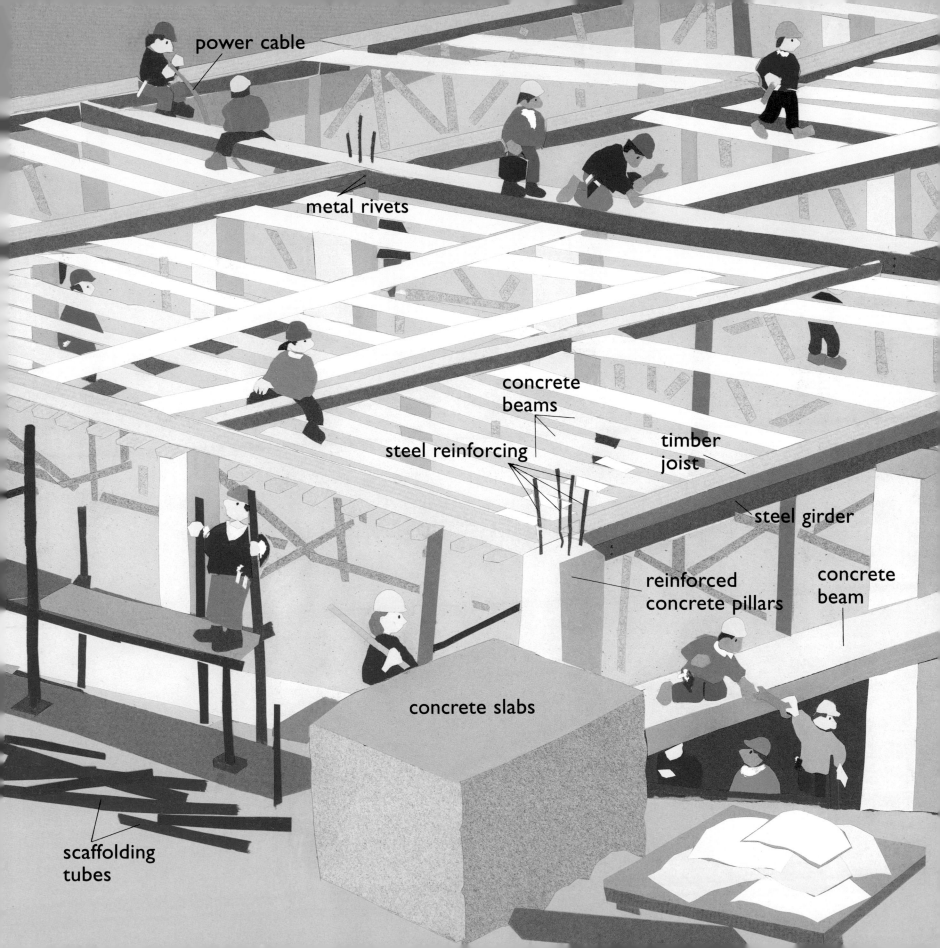

power cable

metal rivets

concrete
beams

steel reinforcing

timber
joist

steel girder

reinforced
concrete pillars

concrete
beam

concrete slabs

scaffolding
tubes

Don't look down!

The skeleton is finished. This is the top floor
of the building. Now the workers will start
to build outside walls. For this stage of construction,
the workers install a temporary elevator and set up
ladders so they can go from one level to another.

steel
girder

construction
site cabin

flatbed
truck

tower crane

tower crane

metal cage elevator

steel cables

pulley

hook

steel cable

wrenches

steel girders

plans

cable

steel girders

metal rivets

protective face shield

power cable

power drill

timber joists

steel reinforcement

steel girder

tower cranes

steel girder

timber
platform

concrete
slab floor

protective
boots

plans

steel trowel

steel trowel

pulley

steel cable

Floors down, ceilings up!

The workers make floors and ceilings.
They spread cement with steel trowels
over a base of sand and concrete.

rubble

dump truck

wet cement

skip

cement mixer

wet cement

wet cement

Up on the roof!

The outside of the building is almost finished. Tower cranes hoist window frames into place. Workers unroll telephone, electric and computer cables.

cable

wooden planks

computer cable

metal cage elevator

wooden strut

plans

wooden struts

electric power drill

electric power drill

computer cable drum

sheet of plaster board

sacks of insulation

computer cable

sheet of plasterboard

architect

blueprints

Saw, hammer, drill!

When the wiring is completed, the electricity can go on. Workers put up wooden struts, and nail sheets of plasterboard to them. Now there are walls and rooms.

plastic tubing around electric wire

telephone cable

air conductor pipe

plumbing pipe

wooden door

plastic tubing for plumbing

faucet

roll of carpet

air conductor pipe

ceiling panel

electric cable

roll of insulation

electric cable

cable junction boxes

steel cable

electric cables

plaster board walls

Room at the top

Pipes are installed that will allow for central air and running water. Then doors, carpets, and ceiling panels are put in. And bathroom fixtures, too!

sink

toilet seat lid

elevator shaft

insulation

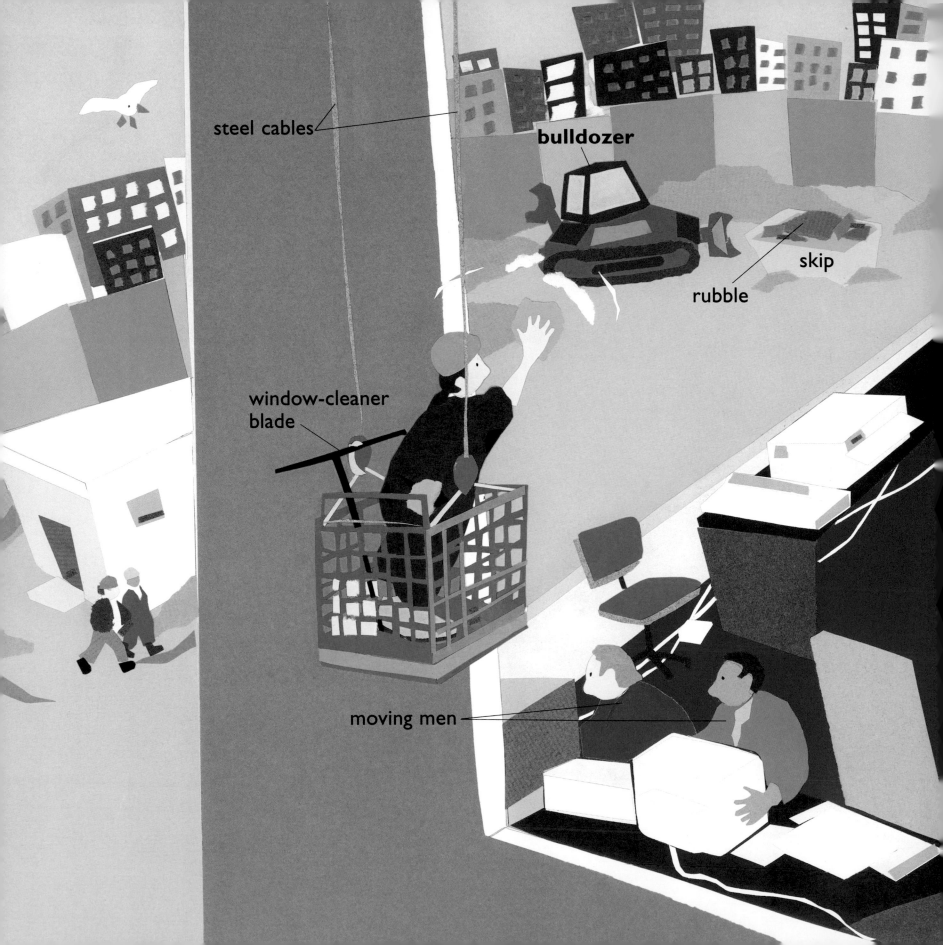

Moving in!

Moving men bring the office furniture. Decorators hang last-minute wallpaper. Now it's time to clean and polish.

decorator

wallpaper paste

sponge

wall brush

decorator

moving men

carpet underlay

carpet fitter

Done!

The building is finished! It's opening day, and the owners give speeches while the office staff listen. They are ready to start working in their new building. Hooray!

traffic jam

Welcome!

the owners

dump truck

cab

mud guard

bulldozer

cab

blade

crawler tracks

hook

mobile crane

boom

cab

outrigger

excavator

cab

loader
bucket

dr

bit

flatbed truck

cab

mud guard

Property of:
Center for Children / Young Adult Books
College of Education
Mankato State University
Mankato, MN 56001